The Adventures of Waggy Tail

Waggy Picks a Family

By Ed Kitsos

I lie at the shelter and
watch people walk by.
I stay far in the back
while other dogs run up
to say hi.

They want to go home
with the first family
they see.
But I want to find a family
as special as me.

I dream of a family
that loves me with hugs.
Who scratches my ears
and gives belly rubs.

I will stand guard at night
because that's what dogs
do.
I will give lots of kisses
because I'll love them
too.

I imagine a big yard
where they throw me
a ball.

And they give me a name so I can come when they call.

I look forward to the day
that my new family
is discovered.

Until they show up
I will stay under
these covers.

Why is this taking
so long?
Seems like I've
been waiting a year.

Will I ever find them?
Will they know that
I'm here?

A few mornings later,
my hopes turning grim.
From under my blanket
I see a family walk in.

A mom and a child.
A boy about five.
There is something
about them.
Did my family arrive?

The boy's very playful.
The mom's patient and
sweet.
Could this be my family?
It's time that we meet.

I let out a yelp
as I make my debut.
I look at the boy
and he looks at me too.

I bark a hello.
I wag my tail
and bark more.
The little boy
comes closer.
He touches my paw.

I can tell by his face
this is where my
search ends.
We'll grow up together
and he'll be my best
friend.

I found my new family.
How do I make them
choose me?

Do I sit nice and still?
Or do I bark,
"pick me?"

I can't control
my excitement.
I jump all around.
I roll on the floor
and make all kinds
of sounds.

The boy calls to his mom
as he points and he claps.
"I want the golden puppy.
The one on her back."

His mother comes over.
I stand tall and grand.

Mom reaches for me.
I rub my nose on her
hand.

She gives me a smile
as they open the gate.
The boy scoops me up.
I knew it was fate.

We get into their car
The boy holds me
real tight.

He looks at his mom,
"Can she sleep in
my bed tonight?"

I start licking his face.
My puppy heart fills
with joy.
I just can't believe
that this is my boy.

My boy and his mother
talk about all the dogs
in the pen.
They think they picked me,
but I really picked them!

As we ride home in the car,
Mom suggests names like Lady and Vail.

My boy shakes his head
"no" and shouts,
"She's my Waggy Tail!"

ACKNOWLEDGMENTS

I want to thank all the people that helped me in this creation of this book: Phil Reyes, Stacey Black, Katie Black, Janine Pekora and Cristina Wojdylo. Without your help, I would not have been able to translate my ideas into a finished product.

A special thanks to Waggy Tail, who not only inspired me to write this book, but who has made my life more interesting since the moment that she picked me to be part of her family.

Meet the real Waggy Tail!